By Colleen E. Jones

Illustrated by Mary Bausman

Interior Art Credit: Mary Bausman

Archway Publishing books may be ordered through booksellers or by contacting:

Archway Publishing
1663 Liberty Drive
Bloomington, IN 47403
www.archwaypublishing.com
1 (888) 242-5904

ISBN: 978-1-4808-6038-4 (sc)
ISBN: 978-1-4808-6040-7 (hc)
ISBN: 978-1-4808-6039-1 (e)

Library of Congress Control Number: 2018908585

Print information available on the last page.

Archway Publishing rev. date: 7/24/2018

I thank my Heavenly Father for the gift of imagination.

I thank my husband, Steve for encouraging me to trust in God and follow His guidance.

A special thanks to my father-in-law, Ken Jones, who spent many summers taking us on camping trips and teaching his grandsons about trees, flowers, and birds. "Thanks Dad!"

When I was a little girl, I would come home from school and tell the most wonderful stories that never happened. Wanting to teach me not to lie, yet allow me to use my imagination, my sweet mother came up with a plan, a compromise. I was allowed to tell my wild stories as long as I began them by saying, *"Once upon a time."* This phrase would let my mother know that I was not lying, simply pretending. So... shall we begin?

Once upon a time
in a tidy nest-
on a strong branch-
attached to a tall tree-
in the front yard-
of a quiet neighborhood-
lived a small bird
named Monica.

Monica loved to sing! She sang many different songs about many different things. In the early morning, she sang the song of the robin. It was a beautiful song that spoke of the sun coming up and dew glistening on the grass. In the afternoon, she enjoyed singing the sweet sounds of the turtledoves. Their song was all about love and peace.

While flying, she often sang a song about the breeze ruffling her feathers. She learned this exciting song from the skylark. Late at night, she sounded just like a nightingale. The nightingale sang a gorgeous song about clouds, quietly drifting through the evening sky. Monica felt that each part of the day and each activity had a corresponding song to go with it. She sang them all!

There was a problem, though. The Robin family didn't like it when Monica sang their song. Mr. Robin said it was a family heirloom and she shouldn't be singing their special song. When Monica sang the Turtledove's song, Lady Turtledove complained. She had written it for her husband, and she felt it was rude for Monica to sing it.

Skylark was one of the few birds who didn't complain when Monica sang his song. Instead, he swooped and darted at Monica and chased her right out of the sky. The sleepy Nightingales didn't even realize that Monica sang their song. They were ever so quietly tweeting with their eyes closed, and they thought Monica was one of them.

Monica was a mockingbird. Mockingbirds are supposed to sing everyone else's song. Still, she often dreamed of singing a song that no other bird knew.

One day Monica heard a sound that she didn't recognize. She decided to investigate. She followed the song to a big green house. Inside was a small human, making a song come out of a big, black box. It was a wonderful song that had many notes flowing up and down from high to low. As she perched in the window, Monica began to sing along with the music. Suddenly, the music stopped and the small human yelled,

"Mom, I can't practice my scales with that bird making such a horrible racket!"

Just then, a larger human came into the room and shut the window right in Monica's face.

Horrible racket! Horrible racket? That human called Monica's singing a horrible racket! Monica cried so hard that she could hardly see to fly back to her tree. Once she reached her nest, Monica decided that she would never sing another note.

After three days of silence, Monica did not feel well. Worms seemed to taste sour, even the plump, juicy ones. She had a stomach ache, and her wings felt weak. The next day, when Monica had a pain in her chest, she decided it was time to go to the doctor.

Dr. Wise Owl examined Monica from beak to tail feather and found nothing wrong with her. When he asked to hear her singing voice, Monica explained that she had given up singing.

"I see," said Dr. Owl. "This is why you feel sick. You know, Monica, birds were created to sing. If you don't sing, you'll continue to feel poorly."

The doctor took out his prescription pad and wrote something on it. He handed the paper to Monica.

"If you follow these directions, you'll get well again".

When Monica returned to her nest, she read the doctor's prescription. It said, "Take a trip. Find a song."

Monica had never been more than a few miles from her tree. She didn't know where to go. She decided to ask beautiful Snowy Egret, who seemed to come and go from the neighborhood.

Snowy Egret was a very shy and quiet creature, so Monica spoke softly when she asked, "Excuse me, Mr. Egret, sir. I'm in search of a song. Where should I go to find one?"

"Try the beach on the other side of the mountain. They sing different songs there. You may find one you like," he replied.

Just as quietly as he had spoken, Snowy Egret flew off. Without a sound, he lifted into the sky and drifted away.

That night Monica ate a healthy dinner of grubs to fortify her for the long flight ahead. After a good night's sleep, she was ready for a new adventure. Before she left the neighborhood, Monica sang the song of the robin. Even though she could see the Robin family scowling at her from the next tree, her chest pain went away as she sang.

The flight to the beach took two full days. At night, Monica found a tree to rest in and tried to sing a bit. By the time she got to the beach, she was exhausted. Monica sat on a large rock and saw the powerful ocean for the first time. She felt the cool breeze and tasted the salty air. She listened very carefully for a song.

A shrill, peeping sound came from a small bird, running up and down the sandy beach, close to the water. Monica went to investigate. She tried getting the funny little birds to hold still and speak to her, but they just kept running back and forth. Occasionally, they stuck their strong, thin beaks into the sand. Finally, one of them stopped just long enough to explain that they were sandpipers, looking for tiny crabs in the grains of the wet sand.

"Try one," the little bird squeaked, tossing Monica a tiny creature before continuing to sprint down the beach.

Monica was hungry and thankful for the food. She tried to catch a few more crabs, but she was not fast enough to catch the tiny creatures. Besides, she didn't like how dry and crunchy they were. The Sandpipers didn't actually sing a song. They just kept chirping the same word over and over again: "Crab, crab, crab." Monica decided to move on.

Overhead, Monica saw many birds that swooped high and low in the sky. They even came close to the giant waves as they flew. As she listened to their song, she heard stories of stealing food from humans picnicking on the beach. Plundering garbage cans seemed to be one of their favorite pastimes. They sang pirate songs about ships and sails and adventures at sea. "Seagull" was their species name, and their days were filled with danger and excitement. Listening to their song and story was great entertainment for Monica, but it was not a song she wanted to sing.

As Monica flew away from the beach, her stomach ache and the weakness of her wings increased. She needed to rest. Just then she saw a large group of pine trees. The trees seemed to go on and on for miles. "This must be a forest," Monica thought. "What a lovely place to rest and find food."

There were worms, insects, and berries galore in the dense woods. She hardly had to search at all to find more than enough food. There were also many birds among the tall, strong trees.

Monica stayed in the forest for several days and learned many new songs. The woodpecker was a fascinating bird with his peck, peck, pecking on the tree to find just the right bug that he wanted to eat. He had a very strong beak, and his song told everyone how proud he was of it.

The oriole was hard to find until he decided to flash his bright orange chest and sing a song about all the colors of the rainbow.

Madam Crow would fly near the tops of the trees, and all the forest creatures could hear the wind rushing through her powerful wings. She sang of strength and wind and speed.

Monica loved the song of the western tanagers. They tweeted a lovely tune about the stately trees of the forest. They educated all who listened about the differences between the ponderosa pine and the Jeffrey pine. Monica learned that the Jeffrey pine smells strongly of vanilla when you fly near it.

She didn't like the blue jay at all! He sang about stealing other birds' eggs. He was a thief, and Monica would not include one note of his song into her collection of music.

As she sang bits and pieces of each song, she grew healthier and stronger. Monica put together all she learned into a song of the forest.

"Why am I still not satisfied?" Monica wondered. "I have filled my repertoire with amazing sounds and practiced them until they blend beautifully together."

She knew that something was missing. None of the songs were her own; she was just borrowing them. So, Monica decided to go home.

As she got closer and closer to her own nest in her beautiful elm tree, she realized how tired her wings were. Monica decided to rest on the high point of a building just ahead. "Perhaps if I take a short nap, I can make the rest of the trip home before the sun sets," she thought.

Monica was awakened by an amazing sound. She flew down from her perch to see who was making it. As she peeked in a window, Monica saw many humans singing together. There were tall humans and short humans. There were humans who looked like they had lived a long time, some who were very young, and every size and age in between. All of them were singing the same words. Monica didn't have to strain to hear what they were singing about because they sang joyfully with loud voices.

The humans sang about a father in Heaven, called God, who loved them. They sang another song, which said, "God created the universe and everything in it". One song mentioned that this amazing God even cared about birds and flowers.

Monica felt her own heart fill with joy. God cared about her! A feeling of love overwhelmed her and she couldn't help but sing about that love. This was a new song! A song that came from her own heart and spoke of her love for God!

As she flew the rest of the way home, Monica practiced her new song. It was a song of praise to her creator, her God, her heavenly Father. It was lovely!

Monica's neighborhood became quiet as she flew in, and perched on her limb. The Robin family, the turtledoves, the skylark and the nightingale stopped their singing and chirping to listen to her song. When she finished, all was still and Monica saw that the birds had bowed their heads, out of respect. She realized that the respect was not for her, or even for her song, but for the One she sang about. It was for God, the creator, who loves us all. Monica had found her own song, but more importantly, she had found the One who created her to sing.

Bible Truth: The story of creation is found in the beginning of the Bible. In Genesis 1:23 we learn that God created birds on the fifth day.

Genesis 1:21-23 (ICB) So God created the large sea animals. He created every living thing that moves in the sea. The sea is filled with these living things. Each one produces more of its own kind. God also made every bird that flies. And each bird produces more of its own kind. God saw that this was good. God blessed them and said, "Have many young ones and grow in number. Fill the water of the seas, and let the birds grow in number on the earth." Evening passed, and morning came. This was the fifth day.

Wonderful Words: An heirloom is something special that is handed down from a grandparent or parent to a child. Some families have jewelry, pictures or books that have been in their family for many years. In this story, the Robin family had a special song that was their family heirloom.

One meaning of the word repertoire is; a list of songs that someone knows and is ready to perform. Monica learned many songs; therefore, she had a large repertoire of songs to sing.

Fun Facts: Mockingbirds can learn up to 200 different songs! The male Mockingbird sings more, and sings louder than the female. They sing throughout the day and into the night.

The ponderosa pine tree and the Jeffrey pine tree look a lot alike. You can tell them apart by their pine cones. The cones of the Jeffrey are gentle in your hand (Gentle Jeffrey). The ponderosa pine cones are prickly (Prickly Ponderosa). Also, the bark of the Jeffery pine truly smells like vanilla.

Snowy egrets have yellow feet. They use their brightly colored feet to stir up, and attract fish, frogs, worms and insects. With quick reflexes and pointed beaks, the egrets can catch their food while standing, walking, running or hopping.

CPSIA information can be obtained
at www.ICGtesting.com
Printed in the USA
LVHW07s1745020818
585751LV00023B/288/P